Snippets

Colleen Seegers

Snippets

Pokeberry books may be purchased for book club, educational, business, and promotional use. For information, email your request to editor@pokeberryexchange.com.

ISBN 978-0997227635
FIRST EDITION

Printed in the United States of America
Cover by Roland Cook
Book Design by Stephen V. Ramey

Acknowledgement

First of all, I want to thank all the people in my life that said, "You should write a book. "The people I owe so much to are the wonderful people in my writers group. Steve Ramey who encouraged me when I thought not one more word could come out of me. His wonderful wife, Sue Linvlle with her kindness and never-ending ideas. How could I not thank Dave, Kathy, Jere, Tim and Tom for their support? They make every meeting of the writers group so much fun with all their pearls of information and advice. And, of course, my deepest thanks to George for his constant support.

Thank you.

Contents

Introduction

This collection of stories has been ruminating in my brain ever since I can remember. I have always loved funny stories. Life is full of them. Some of these stories took on a life of their own, going in directions that surprised my imagination. I hope they make you smile.

Picnic

When you get invited to a long–standing picnic—you know the kind—Aunt Barb always brings the beans and Mary makes coleslaw and the hostess says, "Oh just bring anything," you know you have a tough crowd to impress. On these occasions I rack my brain to think up some very pretty and unusual dish that has never shown up at this particular picnic. Then my limited talents come to the forefront and most of the ideas involving sparklers and volcanos just fizzle into a growing sense of dread.

But this year a pop–up on my computer promised a flag cake that was easy and would wow. I read the directions and knew this was to become my claim to fame. Five layers with the handy use of cake mixes and bought icing. Who would guess that little secret? It would be a time consuming, but I had been a single mother with a full– time job in my pre-retirement life, so this was a go.

With the ingredients lined up on the counter, production began. My son was visiting and planned to update my TV and computer while I did the baking. It seemed like a great idea, but soon he was asking questions as I measured water and oil. Then I had to answer some additional queries from tech support on the phone before pressing forward with my quest for picnic glory.

The batter had a skimpy look in the pans so I did some math in my head about three times before the light bulb in there burst into flame. I didn't add enough water. With all the care of wiping a chapped baby bottom, I extracted batter from the pans, set the mixer on Super Burst and blended in the water. The next three layers came out perfectly, if being lopsided doesn't count.

Then came the assembly. I re-read the directions and decided they had made a mistake. *An easy fix*, I thought. When the cake was half assembled, there was that light bulb again. My new plan for stacking layers had a big flaw, but if I took the cake apart now it would crumble. Regrouping, I made the cake four layers instead of five. We innovators must be flexible after all.

Even with four layers and some shaving here and there, the poor thing was top heavy and getting ready to tumble before it was in the car for the drive across town. Bamboo sticks worked great. Crisis averted.

When the cake was cut, it looked so pretty and there were *ooohs* and *ahs* that nearly matched my ambitious expectation. After a few cuts, though, the bamboo had to come out. An avalanche ensued. *Ooohs* and *ahs* transformed to *Ohs* and *nos*. Thankfully, the hostess was so gracious. She whisked my cake inside, cut it down the middle, and it was almost as good as new.

Next year I think I'll take paper products.

Clothes

I have been thinking of clothes a lot lately. Must be the ton of laundry I do every week. Did I mention I love clothes? Vowing not to buy a thing for two months, I always cave in and give myself a very valid reason to purchase something on sale. (*It won't be there when I need it; what a great present it will be* is some of the logic I use.) Telling myself that I am doing the earth a favor when I shop at resale shops gives me a good feeling. The world has a few more things that don't end up in the trash thanks to me.

I do get uneasy when wearing one of my "finds" and someone comments they used to have a dress like that, "a long time ago." Do they recognize the garment as theirs, or are they telling me it's out of style? If I know this person may be at a function I attend, I will avoid *all* of my resale clothes, which kind of defeats the joy of the great price and what I know is a good look.

I have been thinking about style trends and the cycles of ten– plus years that seem to characterize them. If only we could keep all the outfits we've bought. Alas, it wouldn't work because our shape changes with time even if we weigh the same. Plus, we would need a half-dozen storage lockers to tuck all those clothes and shoes and hats into. And, of course, the type of material and the color, prints or stripes, leave a tell-tale clue to their age that doesn't quite match the new version of the style. Nothing is funnier than someone trying to be a bygone hippie, who has totally missed the mark. No hippie wore creased jeans and perfect–length shirt and beads.

This fashion dilemma can be partially solved by becoming a nudist. You need only a few basic cover–ups in public and no storage lockers at all. On the other hand, this encourages a whole new mindset for broaching other potential social gaffes and ways to think about "stuff." In all honesty, I don't think it would solve a thing for me!

The Perfect Man

I thought I met the man of my dreams at a party one afternoon. He was handsome, a doctor, very charming and funny to talk to. He knew a lot of the same people I knew and I thought, *if nothing else, my boring social life was going into full gear.*

We started dating on a fairly regular basis. He was from Mexico City and spent a lot of time in Tijuana. I loved going to the many cultural events and restaurants there and meeting his friends, though I was at a disadvantage due to my limited Spanish. My dream man did not like to translate and many times he gave me the less–than– Reader's–Digest condensed version, or even told me there was no English word for what they were talking about. He would change the subject and make me think I was being pushy.

Within six months, I began to see Mr. Perfect's flaws. "Don't you have any snacks and some wine?" he would say after I had dressed for an evening out. "We could just watch this great show coming on TV." Sure, that's okay from time to time, but twice in two weeks was getting kind of old, especially when he added, "Is this the only wine you have?" and, "What other snacks do you think you can get?"

If I had him over for dinner he would say he had never eaten whatever I made and grill me about the ingredients. Then he would start to eat and say, "Where is the meat?" or, "Why did you put cheese in this?"

"You said you never ate this before. How do you know it's supposed to have meat and not cheese?" The surprised look he gave at my boldness and the snickers from my kids would soon have him insisting that every combination dish must have meat. He would remember one of his friends or an acquaintance talking about how this recipe always had meat and whatever else he thought I left out.

Then he got a chance to go to South America and Machu Picchu for a conference. He was so excited when he came back, especially since Shirley McLaine had been filming there about ancient people and one of her past lives. It was going to be a TV special in a few months. He talked about it all the time and how sorry he was that he could not get very close to the filming or talk to Shirley. As the show date approached, he reminded me again and again to be sure to watch.

The night the special aired, I was very busy and totally forgot. The next day almost as soon as I got home from work, he called. "What part of the show did you like the most?" I was a little embarrassed. "I was so busy yesterday I forgot to watch." Long pause.

"What was your favorite part?" I could not believe what I was hearing. "I didn't see any of it." Another long pause. "You didn't see any of it?" I thought, *what is the matter with this man?* He then asked again, "What did you like the most?" When I repeated that I didn't see any of the show, he seemed to finally get it. The conversation ended.

Several days later I saw him in person and he gave me some earrings he got in South America. They were very pretty blue stones. He beamed, saying they were to match my eyes.

I have green eyes.

When I mentioned that fact, he brushed it aside and switched to a new monologue about the trip. I began to see how things weren't going so well in our relationship.

One day we were sitting on the couch at my house and conversation seemed to be flowing very smoothly. We had lots of laughs until I suggested that one of his claims seemed very unlikely."I think you're pulling my leg." He looked startled, stared at my legs, and drew himself up as tall as he could (he was short). "I wasn't even touching your leg." I tried not to laugh, but could not contain myself. That seemed to confuse him even more. Explaining my comment only made it worse, so I just said, "It's okay."

We began to see less of each other. I was sure he had a medical condition, and I think he believed I was his nightmare.

About two years later I encountered him in a grocery store. He was so sweet, offering a hug and kiss, and telling me how wonderful I looked, and how was everything? We engaged in some light conversation before he got serious. "Something happened to me, and I don't know how it happened. I got married about a year ago."

I wish I could have met his wife!

The Experiment

Today is going to be a really cool day with a new way to have lunch with my good friends from California. We're going at the same time to the same restaurant in different cities and call each other. In that way we will be together. As hesitant as I am to leave my demon cat home alone, I am thrilleld at the prospect of eating with my pals like we usesd to before I moved away.

So I go to the restaurant and am so excited I wolf down my soup like I was starving while waiting for the jingle. Three–fifteen, nada, three–thirty, nada. It's now noon where they are and that restaurant is always hopping. I figure they're waiting on me, even though the agreement last night was that they would sit together and call me when they were ready to order. Unfortunately, I don't have the cell number in my phone for a goofy reason I'm not going to 'fess up to.

Finally, I leave the restaurant at 4 to do some shopping and they call me. Seems they've been calling my home phone and leaving messages. They offer up many "I'm sorry's" for the error, then one adds that I should get younger friends. We share a good laugh and decide to try the lunch thing again next week. I will have the cell number in my phone for sure that day.

As I'm hanging up, the pain–in–the–ass cat knocks down a wonderful bag I keep out because it's cute and I love it. Then he proceeds to highjack it out of the room. I think he's planning to pack it with his toys and run away to his friends. Maybe he'll call when he gets there.

I hope he doesn't have my cell number.

The Grocery Store

Anne walked into her bedroom to find her four-year-old daughter sitting at her prized vanity, which was now covered in Flaming Pink lipstick. Haley smiled up and announced, "Look how pretty I am, Mommy." Anne stifled a scream, counted to five, and managed a weak, "Wow." How was she going to get the antique mirror and vanity back to its pristine status? She clenched her fists and thought of how she had had to make budget adjustments and sell her husband on the benefits of her spending less time in the bathroom each morning thanks to this lovely vanity.

"How about a fun bubble bath and then we'll get some lunch?" She took Haley's little lipstick–covered hand and went down the hall to the bathroom. While the tub filled, she removed Haley's clothes . Into the trash can they went. No way all that mess would wash out.

With Anne's assist and Haley's hop, Haley was in the suds, scooping up bubbles and talking to herself. Kneeling by the tub, Anne got Haley cleaned in no time. Afterward she helped her daughter dress and the two of them headed to the kitchen to get two toasted cheese sandwiches going and some crisp apples cored and sliced. While they ate, Anne talked about needing to ask before using anything in Mommy and Daddy's bedroom. Haley wasn't too impressed. She squirmed in her chair and asked if she could play with her Barbie. Anne sighed "OK" as she piled plates into the dishwasher.

She glanced to the family room where her curly–haired daughter was busy with Barbie in her pink car having a great time. As she walked back to her bedroom, Anne considered the need to clean the vanity, a gloomy chore if there ever was one. Haley didn't take naps anymore, so Anne would need to limit her cleaning time in order to make sure Barbie was keeping her daughter out of any more trouble.

With lots of elbow grease and several soft cloths, the linseed oil showed promising results. Anne peeked in on her daughter. Haley was now coloring pages in her book while giving instructions to Barbie on what to do next. She had to cover her mouth to keep the chuckle from being audible.

"Haley, do you need a drink of juice?" Haley nodded. "Oh sure!" They headed hand-in-hand to the kitchen.

While they sipped the tart juice, Anne reminded Haley of the need to respect things that were not hers. "You would be sad if I played with your Barbie and tore her dress. Please remember to ask before you try new things that aren't yours." This time the talk had more impact. Haley nodded and turned to look at Barbie lying on the family room floor. Anne considered what to make for dinner. She would need to go to the store. A quick touch of lipstick, a brush through her hair, a wipe of Haley's face, and off they went in the car.

The store was very busy with mothers pushing carts up and down the aisles. Haley was a little upset with being put in the shopping cart, but otherwise Anne would be chasing her all over and making her put back things they didn't need from shelves within her reach.

As they rounded an aisle, a middle-aged woman started talking to Haley while rubbing her arm. Anne smiled, but felt uneasy with all the touching. "Thanks for your kind words," she said, "but we're in a hurry." The woman smiled and nodded, but remained in place as if glued to the floor.

At the checkout, Anne looked for the woman, but failed to see her anywhere. She didn't know whether to be relieved the woman was gone or worried that she had simply disappeared.

No sooner had they exited than Anne was startled by a cheery "Hello." The over-attentive woman stood by the door grinning and reaching for Haley. The hair on the back of Anne's neck stood. Something wasn't right.

"Do I know you?"

The woman smiled and shook her head "no" then did a shoulder shrug of "maybe." Anne grabbed the shopping cart and shoved it, one wheel wobbling, to her vehicle. She strapped Haley in the car seat and looked around before she loaded bags into the back seat. No sign of the woman. She left the shopping cart beside the car, something she never did, and drove for home as fast as she could.

Haley laughed. " Mommy, I like it when you go fast."

Anne caught her breath and slowed down. What if she got pulled over? Would the cop believe her? Was she overreacting? What should she do?

When they arrived home (safely, thank God), she got busy fixing dinner while keeping Haley entertained with cartoons. By the time Bob came home from work, the strange woman was a distant memory. They talked about weekend plans and what to do about the vanity. Not all the lipstick had come off and a section of the finish wasn't as shiny as it had been.

Bob played with Haley and had her laughing and rolling on the floor while Anne cleaned up. When she finished, he had already put Haley to bed. They had just sat down to watch some TV when Anne recalled the lady at the store.

He brushed it off. "Probably some lonely woman wishing she had a cute kid like ours. You worry too much. It was just one of those things." Anne nodded. She had to put it out of her mind.

The next day she and Haley were out mailing a package, when she thought she saw the woman. Holding her daughter's hand tighter, they hurried to the car. On the drive home, Anne kept taking deep breaths and trying to relax.

When she pulled into the driveway, the woman was standing on the front porch, smiling and waving. Her lips fairly glowed with flaming pink lipstick.

Anne called the police and waited in the car.

Storms

I am afraid of storms, but when they happen I have to check on them. I peek out windows, move the blinds very delicately as if the storm will know I am spying. Trees are always a concern to me. What if they fall on the house? What if the road gets blocked and I can't get out? The phone might not work, the power will fail, I'll get cold, the food will spoil. Those things have not happened to me in a long time (and only in other parts of the country) and got remedied very quickly. Nonetheless, when thunder starts and wind howls, I get out flashlights, candles, matches, blankets, canned food with flip tops and bottled water. I become a miniature disaster team. When the storm passes, I'm always so happy. I put the evidence of my fears away as fast as I can, so no one will know.

This week I had two days of ambition. The sun was out, the air warm and I was so energetic. Things outside got swept, old leaves got picked up, I talked to my emerging plants. I even took a chair out to the patio and sat in the sun to read. The next-door neighbors felt it too. They were on their patio, smiling as they scrubbed. Do I need to say what happened next? The temperature dropped, the sun vanished, the wind howled, and I nearly ran inside to prepare for the worst.

The New Princess and Her Unsolved Problem

Once upon a time there was a very successful career woman (she thought of herself as a princess) who loved her job and worked very hard to be the best. She was well liked by her peers and management gave her praise and many perks—you know, like parking and flexible hours.

She kept her appearance without flaw. Her clothes fit perfectly. Any new style could be found in her closet. She had her hair, nails, toes and skin done weekly. Massages were a must with her busy schedule. She was the envy of her friends.

Alas, even with all of the above, there was no prince charming in her life. Men she went out with inevitably liked her, but never called for a second date. She was mystified.

What she never knew—but you and I could hardly miss—was how incessantly she talked on these outings, tuning out many wonderful conversations in the process. She even missed important messages the universe was trying to pass to her.

Years crept by. She reached her final career goal. Retirement. She loved it! Time for the gym, lunches, shopping. She took up golf, learned to judge wine, travelled the world and even gained some recognition for the watercolors she entered in several shows.

It should be added that throughout her hectic life she had been prone to episodes of becoming messy, leaving her house in such a state that her maid sometimes threw up her hands and shook her head in disbelief. Even with this, the princess' smile remained ever present.

One day as she pawed through her crammed closet for the perfect outfit, she discovered that some of her scarves and bracelets were missing. She began to move hangers and shoe boxes, and the closet quickly became very disorganized.

A voice from the universe called to her, "If you build it —"

"Hey," she said, "I don't know anything about baseball and my yard is too small for a field."

The annoyed universe retorted, "Get a grip. You need a bigger closet with more shelves. Lots of things have fallen on the floor. Where did you get the idea about baseball? Call a contractor to help you."

She meekly complied. Later that day a contractor came to assess the situation. He was spellbound by her poise and beauty and wanted to ask her on a date, but she kept interrupting him. He wrote out his estimate and plan for the closet, and left it on a hallway table. There was a note at the bottom asking for a chance to have dinner with her. He left with a heavy heart and a slow walk. She didn't notice the paper.

A week later she was getting ready for a trip and, in her frustration to pack, threw so many clothes out of her closet they landed in the hallway on top of the note from the contractor. To head off her maid's imminent resignation, she very sweetly asked if the dear woman would please pick up the clothes and shoes and purses and donate them to charity. The maid stared open-mouthed. No one, least of all her, knew whether her shock was from the mess the princess had created, or the consideration for others she had shown.

The maid, now grinning ear to ear, scooped items into a very large box, not realizing the contractor's note was lanced on the heel of a stiletto. To this day the contractor waits like a lovesick puppy by his phone, though he *has* received several closet jobs from thrift store customers who may not have the calves for stilettos, but cannot resist a peek at a secret note.

Two Stories and a Meeting

It was dusk, that time when shadows play tricks with your mind. For the man walking slowly along the dusty road, it seemed like tricks had been happening all day. Crickets chirped longer and louder than normal, and sudden gusts made the grass sway in patchwork patterns.

The smell of rain was in the air. The man scanned the horizon. A flash of lightning startled him. His forearm froze above his eyes. The tear in his jacket ruffled. He pulled up the collar and bent forward as the wind increased, the sky darkening.

Lightning came in long bursts, unleashing a nearly constant grumble. He looked across the fields and saw trees about a mile away. His pace quickened. He was tired, but being in the open and wet was not something he wanted. Even so, he was only able to walk for short periods before stopping. His breathing became labored. A few drops of rain began and then stopped. He prayed silently for strength to find shelter from the storm.

He had nearly crossed the field when rain let loose in torrents. He made it to the first tree and fell to the ground, panting. It took several minutes for him to calm. He crawled to a spot on the other side of the trunk that gave him more protection from the rain that was now a steady downpour.

§

The morning was hot, humidity at 89%, the flies thick and biting in the animal tent. She was daydreaming about wearing a white coat and being treated with such respect…

"Hey, you have to get this done before showtime and clean yourselif up for the popcorn stand. Get those skinny arms moving"

She blushed and started to shovel manure with a vengeance. She thought, *One more paycheck and I am out of here,* she thought. *I need to get back to college and my dream of being a vet.* This circus thing was such a bad move. Her family didn't know where she was. She would be ashamed if they did.

It was a cliché, joining the circus, especially a broken-down one like this. She hated the trailer she shared with four others, smokers and people with little ambition. She didn't want to hear one more story from *The Enquirer*. She hoped the matinee would be well attended to make the afternoon go fast.

As she started for her trailer to shower, clouds pushed through the sky. By the time she was done, a light rain was falling. She felt a tremor of worry. If attendance wasn't good they might pack up this afternoon and head for the next small town. Packing was such an exhausting process, almost as bad as shoveling manure.

The show was not a complete washout, bleachers maybe a quarter- filled with soggy children and umbrella-toting adults. Afterward, she cleaned and stored the popcorn machine, took down the small tables and other equipment at her station and stowed them away. Leaving in the morning would give her time to plan a goodbye speech for payday. She slid into her bunk without a word and covered her head with the coarse blanket to avoid the usual trailer chatter. Keeping her face to the wall she fell asleep.

§

Before dawn, workers could be heard calling commands and spurring heavy equipment and trucks to life as the circus was compressed into a caravan and started its crawl to the next show. She was upset with herself for not researching the town and the modes of transportation she might find there to begin her journey home.

As morning progressed the rain, which had been intense during the night, tapered to a drizzle, making parts of the narrow, winding road dangerous. The trucks moved slowly through a morning that seemed to drag on forever.

Finally they stopped for lunch and a chance to stretch out stress- tensed muscles. Walking along the road, she saw how the rain had beat down the tall grass. Green leaves littered the pavement. Just as she was turning to go back, she saw the slumped shape of a person near a tree. A feeling of panic came over her; she couldn't bring herself to move closer.

She ran back for help. Several men followed her to the tree, and she stayed back while they checked the man. He let out a groan and sat up. His eyes met hers for only a moment, but it was enough. A shiver of recognition coursed through her. He was a troublemaker who had been fired a few days earlier. The shiver expanded throughout her body, as if she was just now feeling the cold rain of the previous night. This man had been strong and belligerent before he left the circus. Now he seemed deflated, a balloon deprived of its source of air.

"Get some law out here," one of the workers called.

Thankful for something to do, she ran back to have someone call the police.

The Cat

The feline population is either loved or hated, and even cat lovers have their moments. My addition to the family sneaked in by his good looks and the pretense of being of noble linage.

Just about three days in, he couldn't keep up the charade, displaying an insatiable yearning to chew on all objects, living or inert. Apparently, he believed that his ancestry was of termite and goat. The furniture had to be doused with hot sauce and a large squirt bottle was required to provide rehabilitating squirts to the face. Unwilling to be intimidated, he developed the cunning of an espionage agent of the highest caliber, and learned to leap and chew with the swiftness of a cheetah.

When furniture was not available, he discovered that the edges of doors were very tasty. Under threat of being picked up and moved as a distraction from his destructive tendencies, he learned to meow sweetly and roll onto his back with eyes as flirtatious as possible. Then he would nip rapidly at the hand reaching for him and run under a sofa or to some other impenetrable domain.

After these frolics, he would experience episodes of amnesia, returning to tirelessly chew and gnaw even with his face dripping from the squirt bottle. A few swipes of his paw to dry, and he was off to another anarchy. He had no shame. Wrecking every shred of civilized structure was his sworn duty.

He possessed no useful hunting skills, as was evident when a huge spider crawled up his back and across his face as he stretched and watched. What kind of protection was this to me? Yawning is not on the approved list of scare tactics. If I was to become a victim of spider bite I had better keep my gun. And to think that I had once believed the killer instinct was way up on the cat activity scale, along with sleeping and grooming.

Now he has become a proofreader, climbing onto my lap to quickly dispel any snippet of misinformation that flashes onto the screen. He pounces on the keyboard to right the wrong. If this is not successful, his next plan is to jump the connecting wires and slowly pull and chew. I wonder how many teeth a cat needs. Would he miss any that vanished? I know I wouldn't.

Dress Up

All girls like to play dress-up. I had a friend who lived across the street who had an enormous box of discarded adult dresses, hats, purses, shoes and some gaudy necklaces that all the neighborhood girls thought were just wonderful. With our imaginations we added embellishments and were the most glamorous girls in town.

My sister was born toward the end of my dress-up days, and I got the job of keeping an eye on her. My friends groaned when she came with me and sometimes they told us to go home. That changed when we came up with the idea to dress my little sister in some of the smaller clothes. She loved the attention and would cry when we had to leave and give back all the fussy stuff we adorned her with. One outfit I remember clearly was the removable sleeves from a Bo-Peep costume. Some tugging and we could pull them up to her panty edges like pantaloons. I think they cut off her circulation and she would cry after a few minutes. We would search our stash of clothes for something more glamorous. She always smiled when the sleeves came off.

Since my sister was being potty trained, she seemed to constantly need to go to the bathroom. If we went home, I might have to stay there and help with some household chore, so I would come up with a good reason for my friend's mother to let us use the bathroom there. We would tiptoe up the steps with a stern warning not to touch a thing and be back down "right away."

My friend and I would lift her up on the toilet and command her to pee. One time we got interested in something in the bathroom and forgot to hold on to her until we heard a distressed little "Help." She had fallen in and just her head and feet could be seen. We wiped her down and told her not to tell a soul or she couldn't come and play with us again. From that day forward when we took her to a bathroom she never had to "go" again.

Seasons

I get so sad with the change of fall to winter. Short days, the need for so many layers to keep warm, the collection of boots arrayed down my kitchen hallway to dry. There are so many extra clothes to wash, the tights and sweaters, long boot socks and, of course, the sweatshirts.

I miss going up to my camper to sit by a fire through the evening and laugh along with other campers' stories. In the city, neighbors drive into their garages at night and don't come out until the next day. Dog walkers encourage their pets to "pee fast" and scurry back inside.

As I consider these negatives, I begin to think of the fun things that cold weather brings. I bake more in the winter. Soups bubble away in a big pot a couple times a week. Drinking tea in the afternoon while I talk on the phone is a wintertime thing. I don't do that in summer since I'm out weeding or walking. Cleaning closets seems easier in the cold weather.

When I start cleaning, the discoveries are amazing. All the craft projects I started in June and bundled up in frustration now seem a little more do-able. There's nothing like turning on the music channel and getting lost in cutting and sewing. Before I know, my stomach is rumbling and the clock says 7 PM. Time for soup.

Mother Nature comes to the rescue about the time I think, *one more moment of winter and I'll lose my mind*. A few warm days arrive, and winter clothes get washed for stowing away until next year when the snow and icy rain returns. Then the warm days come on in earnest and winter fades beneath a sense of renewed energy as I plan for the coming spring and summer.

Six Entries

I had the scare of my life a little while ago. I was walking into my bedroom and saw the cat napping on my bed and, for a millisecond, I saw two of him. Holy crap! Two. I'm only now recovering from his last nasty slash to my hand. If he had recruited a clone or a twin, I would soon be in the hospital for blood and antibiotics.

§

It's confirmed. I am addicted to TV. I have it on all the time at home. I always say it's for the noise, but I can be sidetracked by some little promo and there I am, sitting, watching, waiting for the next program, or the one at 9 PM, or making a note for the Tuesday special. If I miss something what will be so bad? None of it really matters: the President's speech; the awards shows; the news that is never accurate.

I don't think I can go cold turkey this week since I just started a diet and am hungry and crabby and… let me think of some more excuses.

§

The sleeping cat is now at the door meowing with such longing and sadness. The cat whisperer needs to do an intervention. Maybe for me, not him. Tune in tomorrow.

§

I have missed some days of writing in my diary and have no excuse. I watched the snow all morning and was lucky enough to get my driveway plowed by 9:30 so that I made the 10 AM exercise class. Very proud that I did yoga here yesterday. Twenty minutes is amazing for me with the TV on. Winter has its challenges, the extra clothes, and the forever off and on with the boots and the zippers on jackets that seem to work when you don't really need them and can make you swear like a sailor when it takes 20 minutes of fiddling before they finally will go. You wake with fluffy hair that just needs a few swipes with the brush, then you stick you head outside and "poof " it's glued to your head and has three extra parts. It's enough to make me want to go to the wig shop. I think I have a few more years before I would start putting the wig on sideways, or back too far, or close to my nose. One of my dear friends has already had some episodes of putting her clothes on inside out. I think she is just trying to brag about what size she wears.

§

I have been thinking very seriously of giving the cat away. I'm tired of cleaning litter off the floor. Having a basement or garage was a saving grace for my previous cats. I'm not sure if this is sugar withdrawal or real emotion. I pick him off the counters all day long and when I come home, the tablecloth is usually hanging from one corner of the table and the mail, covered in bite marks, is scattered across the floor. His mother has been smiling ever since he left home. She probably became celibate and works for Planned Parenthood. I hope she is not seduced again by the cad who was Rex's father. I don't even feel bad for making nasty remarks about someone I don't know.

§

I spent the day as if I had no worries, no plan, and just loved every minute. The TV was on with me watching for several hours and then glancing while I cleaned out some drawers and folded laundry. I was relaxed. I phoned an old friend and we talked for almost an hour, the last of the conversation rushed by last minute things we forgot to tell each other earlier. I marveled at the progress my little flower garden is making. The new shoots announcing, "I survived the winter and I can see the sun!" I hope to do the same.

The Plant That Took Over the House

After my family and I had lived in the house for several years we noticed that plants flourished there. Most were on a once–a–week watering schedule and got a little fertilizer twice a year. Some of the leafy varieties were hard to move so I did the lazy thing and vacuumed around them.

I was amazed when I tried to move one of the 20-gallon pots and discovered that roots had grown through the pot's bottom to snake along the carpet and into the padding beneath it. I had to give it the heave–ho and landed on my butt after pulling and tugging. The roots may or may not have gone on their merry way, but they certainly stayed in the carpet.

I noticed that some of the plants seemed to not follow the sun. They leaned into the room as if spying on us. My teenage kids told me I needed more of a life, the answer they gave for most situations. "Oh Mom, you need to get out more."

So, I ignored the strange plants. Sometimes when they looked really distorted I figured my kids were messing with me and resisted reporting my observations because it would be playing into their hands. I'll show you!

I did mention the plants to one of my friends at lunch one day. She reached for my hand and patted it as if I had displayed the beginning of a senile episode. I was shocked. Never again would I talk about these plants that grew and grew and were so shiny and green and had taken over the living room.

With summer coming, vacation seemed a good idea to get us all ready for Fall and school starting up again. Lots of discussion went into where we would go, with a consensus forming—well, my insisting—that it could only be one week due to finances and, of course, to get home and water the plants.

Off we went to New Mexico, a place I had lived in in my younger days. The weather was perfect, we saw some of my old friends, and got to sightsee some of the most amazing features of that rugged landscape. On the way back we stopped to do some clothes shopping.

When we arrived home, I was feeling a great urge to take my shoes off and start going through piled–up mail. Then I entered the kitchen and was stunned by what I saw. I was so scared I told the kids to stay outside. Big mistake. They came charging in and were also stunned, stopping just inside the doorway.

The pantry was partially open, with what looked like a snake peeking out. I reached for the phone to call 911. The snake just stared.

My son moved closer. My breath caught and before I could yell, "Stop!" he was very close to the snake. I wanted to rush into the room and grab him, but my legs were frozen solid despite the hot day.

He turned to me with a grin and said, "Mom, what did you leave in the cupboard?"

It was the stem of a potato going to seed and probably looking for the backyard. We all had a good laugh, and the 18–inch "snake" was ungracefully thrown into the outside trash can. I remain convinced that the living room plants had a hand in coaxing that potato to scare us.

As for *them*—the living room plants—I disposed of them one by one. The last few were donated to a plant booth at our church carnival. What a job to get them out of the car and across the playground. I was returning to my car for a final haul, when a short man wobbled down the sidewalk carrying the plant I had just donated. When he saw me he stopped and said, "Look at this beautiful plant. How could someone give this away?" I didn't say a word, only smiled and thought, *just wait until it follows you around the house and takes over your living room.*

The Quirks of Dinner

When I was growing up dinner was the whole family at five o`clock. My mother was a good cook, her meals balanced and served so every food was hot/cold and ready at the same moment. We kids got the five minute warning. "Go wash your hands and sit down." My Dad made sure the four of us, got the job done. He, on the other hand, would linger in the dining room doorway. He never sat until the food was on the table. If my mother forgot butter he would mention it and wait. This caused her to scrunch her face into a "look". He would take his time sitting and give her a grin.

In summer, we ate lots of fresh things from our garden and local markets. My Dad loved this kind of eating and especially loved to finish a meal with cold watermelon. Oftentimes, he would ask my mother to delay dinner a few minutes while he dashed to the store. "Wouldn't a nice piece of watermelon taste good for dessert?" Off he would go.

Thirty or forty minutes would pass before he returned. At first Mother would gaze out the window to see if he was coming down the street. After twenty minutes or so, she would read the paper with one eye watching. Then he was back, appearing as abruptly as he had disappeared. In would come several bags of things that tempted him in the store. "Where's the watermellon?" one of us would ask. He would look startled, blush, and laugh after mumbling a swear-word admission that he had forgotten the watermelon. More often than not, he wouldn't go back to the store until the next day.

To cover his embarrassment he would tell us stories of the terrible things he had to eat as a boy. "We got dandelions for dessert. We loved them." The older of my brothers and I would roll our eyes. Then the tone changed and he asked about school or friends and how we were. To us that was how dinner was.

The Surprise

It was just a typical day, housecleaning to do. Laundry. So I drank my extra coffee and strolled down the hall. When I opened the closet to get cleaning supplies, a laundry detergent bottle crashed down on my foot. "Crap!" I yelled and started to rub my poor red toe.

There was something at the back of the closet that I had never seen. Moving some bottles of this and that, I uncovered a tiny door. Did the fairies move in or was the mouse I have been trying to catch for months more cunning than I imagined?

I crouched and did some wriggling into that crowded space. The door had a handle! I rubbed my eyes, but the little pink knob was still there. The door opened slowly, revealing a tiny hole.

Sweat beaded. My breath came shallow. I felt like I was going to pee myself. *This is a dream. I'd better go to the bathroom.* But no, I was awake. Scooting further into the closet, I saw light in that hole and heard sounds.

I pressed my eye close. There they were, a tiny man and woman talking and laughing at a table. I didn't want them to see me, but I had to figure this out. I tapped my head against the wall. That would return me to reality.

Then it was back to the tiny door and the tiny people. They were so handsome and polite, and just kept talking and laughing. *What is this?* I put my ear to the opening, but the sounds were so low and fast I couldn't make out a word. For about fifteen minutes I stayed in that position, alternating eye and ear until my legs went numb. I backed out of the closet, gulped some aspirin, and took a nap.

By the afternoon, I had to return to the closet. None of this made sense. Who were these people and why hadn't I noticed the door before? I laid out a thick bath towel and knelt onto it to keep myself more comfortable. *I'm in this for the long haul*, was my only thought. I had outsmarted teenagers, I could figure this out.

The door didn't open as easily this time. It took a tug, and my hand slipped and crashed into the real door jamb behind me. I crammed my fist into my mouth to keep from screaming.

When I finally calmed down, I moved my eye into position. Something was different. The handsome people stood by the table, arms folded across their chests and looking very stern. They must have argued while I was napping. Their conversation continued, but not a word was loud enough to make out.

My mind churned these strange events around, with no answer coming. I decided to yell into the hole to get things started. Just as I got a gulp of air into my lungs and was about to make Tarzan proud, the doorbell rang, followed by pounding and yelling.

I crawled from the closet and closed the door. The doorbell was going nonstop. The banging sounded like the door was on the verge of crashing in. I was afraid to open it. I could barely get out a creaky, "Who is it?"

"Police", came a booming voice. I gripped the doorknob, and slowly turned it.

"You know why we're here," the uniformed officer snarled. "This is the second time you've spied on your neighbors this month. Start wearing your glasses and your clothes or we're going to arrest you."

The Unofficial Story of the Purse

I have always been fascinated by purses. Just a peek in my closet will give you an idea of how easily I could get to collector status and possibly be on the TV hoarders programs to be exposed to all the world. I am sure they are all necessary to complement the variety of outfits I own and to cope with the constantly varying need to carry important and maybe–not–so–important items. Any female can tell you that what you need for shopping at the mall is very different from what is needed for a swap meet. And don't get me started with what accoutrements church, a concert, or dinner with friends and/ or family require. The most thought-provoking challenge is deciding what items to carry to a function where the ex-wife or girlfriend will be checking you out. Nothing but the best will do. The small black Coach bag is always noted.

I won't bore you with the entire history of purses, but some form of this device has been around since man decided he needed a way to take his clutter and can't–live–without items with him. And yes, men carried them first. They gave them up, probably by tricking women into using them—*it makes you look so sexy and, by the way, can you carry this for me?*

Most purse carriers will tell you the design flaws they have encountered over the years and the features they look for in a new bag. I am a compartment person. I like things separate and easy to find. The vast black–hole kind of bags seem out to trick me, usually in a dark movie theater when I need the cough drop or a Kleenex to cope with the most tender moment in the movie. The audience sits, silently glued to the scene, and all you can hear is the rustle and banging around in my purse. I swear I am as quiet as I can be, especially when the dirty looks and *shushes* start.

There should be a Velcro kit in every purse. Quick as a wink you could adhere Velcro to your imperative items and there would be the perfect spot in the purse for the loops to attach. Everything would remain in place, easy to find, but maybe a little noisy. I suppose that over time the Velcro would collect fuzz and hair and lose its usefulness. There would be advantages to that too—the need for a new purse! Got to keep the economy humming someplace on the planet.

Sometimes I am lulled into thinking I can just cram a few things in my pockets and be fine. I have trouble managing a single pair of gloves in my winter jackets; why do I think this will work? The fashion meter flatlines as bulges appear in unflattering places,

Kleenex floats gracelessly to the floor, hands clench zombie-like around those sunglasses I forgot to leave in the car. Makes me want to throw it all out and let the chips fall where they will. This is usually when I feel very naked without my lipstick touch–up, bangs in my eyes, and that shiny nose in the photos that land on the web. Maybe the back–to–nature girls have something after all.

While we're at it, I should tell you that men wore high heels first. That's another gimmick we embraced for the sake of fashion. Thereafter, men smiled and nodded appreciatively when we wobbled past. Their feet felt good for the first time in years.

Big Thoughts on Tiny Houses

I love tiny houses. They are so cute! Things are carefully arranged into every nook and cranny, and steps to the loft that twist and turn, but can still hold your underwear. That 400 to 600 square feet is just genius.

But wait, no one has created a program showing how it is to live in a tiny house for a year or more. I have never seen that confident big guy with his thumbs under his suspenders, grinning into the camera and saying, "Bill, me and the missus have been having the time of our life in this four-hundred-and-fifty-square-foot slice of heaven. We love bumping into each other, and if one of my socks misses the clothes hamper, why we just love the cluttered look."

This makes me wonder what else could be a drawback? Where do you put your Mother-in-law when she visits? Do you sleep in the tent or does she? When it's your turn to host bunko, it had better be warm out and your yard can't have a slope or you are out of the game. Your membership to Sam's Club has to be cancelled since there's only room for one roll of toilet paper. Will your home owner policy only cover the first time you fall out of the loft? *Sorry, you're on your own for the others.* And don't ever get an urge to start a collection that takes up more than one square foot.

Most tiny houses are on wheels and are moved around due to restrictions of city codes they don't meet. When not attached to the truck towing them, they could be stolen. Can't you just see the police chasing that house down some winding road with the curtains flying out the windows and the siding flapping in the breeze?

I don't know about you, but I need to think through this tiny house craze a little more fully before I jump in and get rid of all but one of everything I own.

Things Are Not What They Seem

I remember driving by this block as a little girl and the entire expanse blazed with lights. It was Christmas and the circus rolled together into something I couldn't describe as other than exciting.

I asked my Mother what the pretty place was and she smiled with some sadness. "Rich people go there. We will have to wait a long time for our chance. But maybe you'll get in, Sweetie. Someday. Tell me all about it when you do."

I thought she had a plan and would let me know when we got rich. I didn't ask her about it. She would surprise me when that day came. I imagined tea parties and princesses, fluffy little dogs doing tricks, and very kind grandmothers passing out cookies. I was four years old.

We didn't drive by that block very often, but it remained fascinating to me. When I was six, life took me farther from those magical buildings. My father went on a trip, and I never saw him again. Not much was said to me at the time and as I got older my questions received only vague answers. Father wasn't dead, but as to where he was, well, that was the dark mystery. *He'ss doing top secret work and only my mother knows where he is,* was the story I told my friends at school. It gave me a feeling of being special. I stopped telling that story when I was ten. Nobody believed it anyway.

Just before I turned sixteen, things changed quickly. Mother was no longer so somber, but became talkative. She smiled so much it scared me. We moved to a bigger apartment close to the city center. and once or twice a week, drove by the "magic" block of dazzling buildings. Even twelve years later I remained intensely curious, but now I wondered not only about the buildings, but the people inside. It must be movie stars and royalty going to dinner, having parties and dancing into the wee hours of the night. I would catch my mother looking at me out of the corner of her eye as I strained to get a good look through any window or opening door we passed.

I became brave enough to demand my mother tell me about my father. She went very quiet, wringing her hands and gazing up at the ceiling. As her face tilted down, she cleared her throat and said, "I am having a hard time finding the words that won't hurt you as much as they hurt me. Your father led a double life. He had another family. I was so blind to the clues. When he died, I was finally able to start over. The courts divided funds he had set aside for his children, and it helped me get training and a better job. I put the rest into a trust fund for you, and have paid back every penny that I borrowed."

I cried and hugged her very tightly. My story about top secret work wasn't so far off, after all. That night, I went to my room and tried to remember everything about my father as clearly as possible. I decided that I wanted to meet his other family someday, but not for a long time. Sleep was a lot of tossing and turning, and some very strange dreams.

When I woke, I remembered part of one, and my plan took form. I was going to the magic block with my mother. Every shop would be on our list. I would save every penny from my babysitting jobs and any other windfall that came my way.

Several months later the magical day arrived. I could hardly wait. Imagination and reality were about to collide. "Here we go!" was my shout as we got out of the car.

What I Fed My Brother

When you grow up in a small town and you have a vivid imagination, you start to do things you think will impress your parents. I was always busy at a young age thinking up deeds that would make them burst with pride.

I was four when my baby brother arrived. He wasn't too interesting until he started to crawl. He loved my attention. I was the best big sister. One Sunday morning my parents were upstairs getting ready for church, and I thought I would help clean the house. Why not feed my brother those unsightly cigarette butts from an ashtray that, for some unknowable reason, was on the floor? He ate the first with only a little protest. The next two took some work, and he was crying by the time I got them down. Mother came downstairs just as he started to vomit. I was interrogated and banished to the corner until we left for church.

One warm, sunny, summer afternoon we went to Gaston Park for a picnic. Mother got busy talking with other mothers and told me to keep an eye on my brother. The sand box seemed a safe place to play. My brother was just starting to walk, and the sand would be a nice cushion for his teetering gait. He loved it and was soon throwing handfuls into the air and laughing. I made a friend and told her my brother could eat sand. She was unimpressed until I gave him a spoonful. Wow, he did eat sand! That was all I needed. As my new friend watched raptly, I fed my brother spoonful after spoonful of that grainy dessert. I have no Idea how much he swallowed before Mother came to check on us. She was so mad, and my new friend was no help at all. She started saying how I forced him to eat the sand and made him cry.

My poor brother had sand in his diapers for 2 days. I know this because with every diaper change my mother would say, "This is all your fault."

Almost Done

I am a closet procrastinator. I am guilty of finding a million things to occupy my time, thus avoiding the high priority task that is the number-one-needs-to-be-done-by-noon item on the list.

Let me give some examples. That speck of dust on the windowsill suddenly needs cleaning with the special attachment on the vacuum cleaner, and that, of course, needs cleaning before it can be used. All because I have a short story to write. The topic and the various ways it can be told ruminate in my mind for hours, even the twists and turns and attempts at character change. I get a smug feeling I will remember all this crafty wit my brain has cranked out. And then— *POOF!*—it's gone because I answered the phone and talked to my neighbor too long.

Daydreaming in the tub can make thirty minutes vanish. Ten minutes is all I need to get the magnesium from the bath salts into my skin. This makes the water very silky. So I put in some bubble bath and from a little movement, the bubbles morph into interesting shapes the way clouds do. The map of Texas, some frogs, a cat, it goes on and on. I have come very close to falling asleep. What an awaking that would be at 3 AM in cold water and shivering.

The big time waster is the television. I always think I will watch for ten minutes. Or just the news. Then the announcer tells of some amazing breakthrough, or a new way to clean, or the easiest beauty plan with only kitchen ingredients that will air in twenty minutes. An hour later I'm too tired to jot down a thing.

Maybe I'll take a bath and watch the bubbles...

Triangle

The Lover

I sit toward the back of the restaurant. It gives me a chance to watch Gloria come in. She has the sexiest walk of any woman I know. Men can't help staring but she's coming to me. Look at that dress, so slimming, and just short enough to give those legs lots of exposure. She looks happy. I love when she brushes her hair back like that. Oh, she wore the bracelet I gave her! She sees me. It made her eyes sparkle, and that smile looks like a million. What a hug, I just can't keep my hands off her. I kiss her hands. Oops, we bumped heads. What a lunch this will be.

The Friend

She's just getting her food at the table when Gloria comes rushing in. What's she doing here? Look at her, so smug and that superficial fling of her hair. Who the hell does she think she is? People know she's fooling around with two or even three men and acting like an angel. Please! I can't stand her. She ruined my chances with Arnold, throwing herself at him and making me look bad with all the lies he believed. And then she dumped him. Oh my God! She's meeting Larry. LARRY!!!! How could he be so stupid? She needs to get some new clothes. That dress doesn't do a thing for her. I'll bet Larry is doing something for her. Look at them. Get a room! Wait until I tell people in the office.

Onlooker

This place is so busy. Look at that woman. She seems very intent on something. Her hair's kind of messy. Wonder why she's looking around so much? Oh, that man back there is happy to see her. Look at the smile on his face. Love that bracelet she's playing with. Expensive. She has kind of a sexy walk. A little exaggerated and meant for attention, but she makes it work. I bet they get waited on before me. That's kind of corny, kissing her hands. Maybe they have after–lunch plans. Wow, what an imagination I have. They're probably old friends seeing each other for the first time in ages. They're probably European and its normal for them with that kissing stuff. Okay, where *is* that waitress?

The House

I held my breath. The papers were signed. The house was mine. Still, that tiny voice whispered in my brain. *Is this what you want? What if it doesn't work out? How will you recover your losses?*

I thought of the changes I would make. The house had good bones and would support any number of fun projects to make it really shine. Compliments would roll in from friends and family. I smiled smugly to myself.

The rest of the day was a blur of a quick lunch, unlocking the front door, doing another quick tour with my mind's eye seeing the changes I would bring to this once proud abode. Along the way some not–so–flattering details came into view that I didn't remember seeing but I pushed them out of mind. *This will go fast. I can relax and enjoy the results in a few short months.*

The house and I had a honeymoon. Four hundred here, six hundred there, a new this, a repaired that. All good. A rosy–glow time.

All honeymoons end. Ours (mine?) was over before the first year of ownership. I was sick of looking at fixtures. Lights, rugs, curtains, towels. Who cares if a ceiling fan has three speeds or five?

A kind of hibernation came on strong. I was no longer giddy about rearranging and shining. It became a chore just to vacuum. I went through the motions of smiling when people asked how my projects were coming along. *Status quo* at best, but I pretended I was going great guns.

Gradually I achieved an *aha!* moment. Nothing can be exciting forever. It's a long–term contract. Appreciate even the ordinary and the mundane. Love the house for what it is *and* how it will evolve. Not a honeymoon moment, but an ownership event.

The Air WasIntoxicating

The air was intoxicating with sounds of music, chatter, laughter. Glasses clinked as I started past the private club. It was hard to resist going in and joining the fun. And so, I did. No one challenged me.

Was this the wisest way to end a grueling work week? Would it ruin my weekend? *Who cares? I'm in.* The lights were bright in parts of the room and barely made a shadow in others. It was a big space filled with people. I smelled perfume, tobacco, pot mingled with incense and hard to place food spices.

In the darker places couples mingled intent conversation with touches, kisses, even caresses. A few swayed to a slow sensual music heard only in their heads, eyes locked or closed, but always bleary. Another fifty or so people laughed and drank around an impromptu dance floor while ogling several young couples glazed in sweat and flushed with the glow of being in the spotlight for this brief time.

Occupying the only well-lit corner, near the DJ station, was a buffet in dire need of attention to refills and good old motherly care. The occasional person wandering past was only briefly annoyed by the mess before spearing a morsel or two to sustain them.

An open doorway led to a cluttered kitchen. I could only see one person's arm, but heard them talking…on the phone? Was another person squashed into that tiny space? The conversation was fast–paced and in an unknown language punctuated by laughs and howls. Briefly a few pots and dishes made some noise, but no food came out of that kitchen, nor did the mystery talker check the buffet.

The DJ nodded off a few times, garnering yells from the crowd. Other times he woke with a start as partygoers tried to get songs going on their own. Time seemed to pick up speed as the first hint of dawn shone through the painted windows. Some couples snored from soft chairs while others said their goodbyes and headed for the front door. The mystery person from the kitchen, a woman with manly arms, made a grumpy appearance with a cart and began piling the mess onto it while shaking her head and mumbling. She looked once around the cavernous room and vanished to the safety of her kitchen.

The Roommate Eviction

Over the spring, I started to hear strange noises in my house. They were very brief and varied. When I investigated the places from whence I thought they had originated, they stopped. Once, I walked into my bedroom to sounds of chewing from a basket in the corner. Holding my breath, I pulled the cover off the basket, expecting to find eyes looking back. Panic gave way to relief when the bottom of the basket was all that I saw. Then there was the night I was awakened by some very loud chewing right under the bed. As soon as the light went on the chewing stopped. I did find disconnected pieces from several posters under the bed, but no culprit.

I asked my boyfriend to set traps. He was not very helpful. "You were dreaming," he suggested, among other sage comments. Mouse droppings appeared in the hallway and guest bedroom and he still wouldn't acknowledge that mice had moved in. I did finally persuade him to set a few traps that caught nothing more than dust bunnies.

We spent a good deal of the summer travelling in our camper and I began to forget about my little guests. As summer wound down, however, and focus returned to my house, the noises returned. Watching TV one night, my boyfriend asked what that clink was in the kitchen. I told him it was the fridge, or the light above the stove making funny sounds.

"No, that wasn't it," he said with a look of expectation.

I wasn't about to get into the mouse wars again. If I suggested rodents he would only resist and ridicule. I stayed quiet and stared at the television screen. My boyfriend got up, looked around the kitchen, and forgot about it.

The next day I opened the silverware drawer to find as many mouse droppings as spoons. I was horrified. And mad. I scrubbed the drawer and silverware and went to the store for a different kind of mouse trap. I have always hated the glue traps, which torture the mouse and leave you to deal with the kill. But difficult times call for difficult measures. I bit my tongue and bought several.

I placed one in the kitchen cabinet.

The next night I came home to frantic noises from beneath the sink. I knelt, not knowing whether to feel elated or terrified, and there he was, a scrawny little mouse chewing the edge of the trap to make good on his escape.

Getting him out was tricky, as he was facing me in a very cramped space. I had to use plyers and heavy work gloves. I apologized as I put him in a bucket of water and out of his misery.

I have since set more traps with no results beyond my peace of mind. As for my boyfriend, he still doesn't believe I caught a mouse. He thinks I brought one into the house to show him up. I wonder if that little hardware store sells a larger trap.

A New Sign

I think we are sent signs in many forms that help us connect the dots of the universe.

Last night I needed a few minutes to read before falling asleep, and I picked up a book of short stories by Sue Monk Kidd. These are early inspirational pieces collected in a book called *First Light*. I read about a trip to a botanical garden she took with a friend. They sat on a bench, and a butterfly landed on Sue and began to travel up her leg and then her arm, and onto her friend. At one point she held out her finger and the butterfly stayed there while they spoke to it. The butterfly stayed with the two friends for the rest of the garden tour. This led Sue to do some thinking about how things are connected.

This morning I went to the garage to leave on an errand and there on the inside wall was a butterfly. It's one I don't remember seeing before, brown with a band of orange and yellow on its wings. March is too cold for butterflies. Where did it come from? I heard birds chirping nearby and wondered if it came inside for protection. When I returned, I left the garage door open, hoping it could go back outside (it was warmer then). It stayed in place, wings closed and moving slightly.

Four days later the butterfly is caught in a spider web. During the time it was alive I kept checking on it. I think it was a sign.

Postscript: It is now one year later and butterflies have been appearing in my surroundings more regularly than I can recall. Some just float by, but one settled on my arm as I was reading on the patio. They have landed on the windows and stayed for hours before moving on.

The other day I was getting some items out of the trunk of my car, and in the back window, was a very dead but beautiful white butterfly. I think I will keep watching them until I get the dots connected.

Dream Trip

I had wanted to go to Hawaii for several years, but every time I planned the trip, a monkey wrench got tossed into the middle of it. I was a single parent of two and worked full time, so juggling the details to get the perfect trip took a lot. Getting time off was the big one, followed by child care, scraping pennies together, and the multitude of little details: mail, newspaper, the yard, the neighbors. I try to take a vacation without my children every two years. When I get back after a week apart, we always like each other even more.

Finally, after three years of emergency tonsils, a major car repair, and a roof, I was on my way. Then, at the last minute, my travel mate cancelled. I panicked. I had never gone on a major trip alone.

I had four weeks to decide if this was another false start. At three weeks, I made up my mind to go alone. There would be group tours, days on crowded beaches, and shopping solo is no problem, so why not? As I was talking about this at work one day, a secretary from a nearby department heard and blurted, "I'll go with you. When do you need the money?" I wasn't sure how this would work out. I barely knew her to say, "Hi." After talking to her over the next several days we decided it was a go. I was in high gear. Smooth sailing!

A delay on our first connecting flight made us a little cranky. That was smoothed over by free champagne on the next flight. My budget for this trip was so tight I couldn't afford extra for movie earphones, but I got pretty good at reading lips and guessing, so I enjoyed the movie anyway. Still, an undertow of dread was beginning to build.

The plane landed late, the shuttle bus system was very confusing, and by the time we got to the hotel, no luggage! We went to sleep in our underwear and made plans to buy cheap clothes the next day. At three in the morning a banging on the door woke us with news the luggage had been found.

My new friend was a shopper! We spent almost all of our non-tour time in the open market. I am so glad I'm a pro at window shopping. We both knew people on the island of Oahu and enjoyed some nice dinners and catching up. Then it was off to Maui.

The flight over is twenty minutes. As you board the plane the stewardess asks what you want to drink. While we were taxiing down the runway, she began tossing cans of *Coke* and *Sprite* at the passengers. Fortunately I have quick hands or I might have experienced my first concussion. Was it really *that* important that drinks were served? Would we have become dehydrated in those twenty minutes? I thought it was so funny.

A smooth landing lulled us into thinking our two days would be trouble free. When we got our rental car, it was suggested we take a drive around the island perimeter. The car's hood kept popping up every couple of blocks. Back to the rental office we went. Lots of screaming and glaring, the office people had a huddle, and we got a different car.

Down the road we went only to have the trunk fly open. Rather than endure another encounter with the car folks, we just stopped at every rest area and parking lot to close the trunk and drive on. Annoying, yes, but kind of fun too.

Maui is gorgeous, with thick vegetation, flowers, and the sound of the ocean everywhere. Our drive around the island was going fine, when my friend let out a blood curdling scream that made me swerve nearly off the road. A big cow face peered through the bushes. I recovered and drove slowly past. Behind us, the cow took a stance in the middle of the road, the next vehicle coming to a screeching halt. It could have been worse, we decided.

When we brought the car back, the only concern of the rental office was whether the gas tank was full. Eye rolls over the trunk problem and then, "have a nice day. " The return flight went smooth as silk and arrived on time. Kind of boring, don't you think?

The Honk

Back in the nineteen-seventies I was a newlywed living in the west Texas town of Lubbock. It was a college town with roots in cattle ranches and oil wells. Keeping to the tradition of the early days of cowboys getting dressed up for Saturday nights, everyone wore their finest to the cinema. The movie to see was Love Story.

My husband donned his best slacks and a crisply pressed shirt while I decked out in a glamorous dress, heels, and lots of makeup. We headed out for a warm Saturday night on the town.

The theater was packed. We had to park several blocks away and barely got inside for the opening credits. *Love Story* was a tragic tale featuring a very moving death scene. Everyone was crying, some with heartbreaking sobs.

The man in front of us decided to blow his nose, the most boisterous *honk* I had ever heard. The couple to my right stifled a giggle, and then from somewhere behind us came a yell, "Shut up!" The whole audience erupted in laughter.

On the drive home, my husband and I talked more about the honk than any other part of the movie.

I Could Hear Someone Calling

I could hear someone calling from far away. I wanted to answer, but the words caught in my throat. I concentrated on the smell of the grass my cheek rested upon. It was so clean, and the coolness and soft pillow it made wanted me to stay forever. I let my thoughts drift to a morning of laughter and feeling so happy. I wanted to hold on to that feeling as long as possible.

The voice called again, closer this time, with more urgency. I knew they could see me in the grass. I closed my eyes and hoped they would think I was asleep.

"Hey," was suddenly in my ear. "Get up." Then I felt it. Rain drops landing on me, faster and larger. I stood slowly, grabbed the umbrella I was handed, and walked to the porch.

We sat together in the swing to watch the storm, smiling and holding hands. It was a good morning.

The Tablecloths No One Knows

When you look at linens at a second-hand store, you often see tears, stains, and odd pieces that aren't used much in our informal lives. The ones that speak to me are print tablecloths of the forties and fifties. They feature rich colors and interesting designs.

When I pick one up to check for imperfections, my imagination comes into full play. I see a family around the table, and Little Billy spills food. To avoid a scolding he positions a milk glass or salad plate over the spot, and it isn't found until after the meal. Sometimes the stain can't be removed, or maybe there's a hole where his frustrated mother rubbed too hard trying.

Cigarettes were another culprit. People of that era drank coffee and smoked after dinner, sometimes for hours. No one was in a hurry. I imagine conversation becoming animated, and there goes an ash or two. Mr. Jones and his cousin keep arguing, and no one notices the burn.

Tears along the bottom bring visions of toddler Johnny waiting not so quietly for dinner to begin. He sees food on the table and tries to reach. When he can't, he gives the cloth a tug. Gravy spills. Fido, the family dog, jumps up... you get the picture.

Another danger to linens was young women learning to iron. They trained in that dreaded art with pillowcases, napkins, dish towels and the occasional small tablecloth. Since only one percent like to iron, many holes are from daydreaming girls with an iron in their hand. *Voilà.* Scorch marks, holes, wrinkles that never come out.

A new use for tablecloths recently came to my attention. They can be mixed and matched to make flowing jackets and dresses. It usually takes two coordinating cloths and some imagination, but you can create some truly stunning outfits.

Happy hunting and sewing. See you at the second-hand store. Maybe we'll encounter the practice cloth I ironed as a girl, complete with scorch marks.

Mistaken Identity

I decided to get away for a while and just think. I was being questioned about a fire at the facility where I worked. Just because I was the only smoker on my unit seemed a flimsy excuse to hassle me.

I didn't tell anyone where I was going. The plan was to rent a motel room and just sit and figure out my next action. The bus seemed the best way to leave.

A name popped up on my cell phone's Google map as I prepared to purchase a ticket. New Castle, PA had a familiar, homey sound. It looked like a town that could fit the bill. No one knew me there.

I arrived at 10 AM and had started to collect my suitcase when someone called my name. Again, I heard, "Chris." An elderly lady with glasses that magnified her wide brown eyes was coming at me, grinning.

"Chris, what a surprise to see you. You should have called. When you get that bag, I want you to come home with me and have a nice cup of coffee. I'll call the cousins to come by for lunch. They will just scream with happiness. Hurry. My car isn't much, but we can get there okay. I just got new brakes and the dents add character."

"I don't know who you think I am, lady, but my family isn't from here. Who are you, again?"

"Oh this darn hearing aid. My new batteries are at home. Just talk louder and we'll be fine. You look so good, Chris. You just missed Aunt Nellie. She's off to a convention in Kansas, some kind of stuff with her work. She should retire."

"Wait", I said loudly. "I don't know you. What's your name?"

"The train? No, don't take the train. It's slow. I'll bring you back to the bus station when you leave. You're staying with me. Why didn't you call?"

Suitcase in hand, I followed this odd woman to a beaten blue-grey Ford, trying to think of a good escape plan. She just kept chattering. She wasn't lying about her car. A body repair shop dream. I wondered if I could maybe end this by telling her I was meeting someone. But who? And why?

"Chris?"

There she was, holding the door open. Maybe I should just run. Her hand was on my arm, and that little gal had some power. She pulled and pushed me off-balance, and I thought, *Okay, next stop I bolt.* I half-fell into the car seat. She shoved the suitcase into the back and came around to the driver's side.

She drove very slowly. *What am I getting myself into?* I thought. *Why does this all seem familiar?*

We crunched to a stop in front of a house that was like something from a movie. A little white four-square with flowers all around, frilly curtains in the windows. I was getting scared now. When the proverbial cousins came over, they would want some explaining and my extrication could go either way, laughs and back patting or the police. I should have paid attention to see if we passed a bar. A stiff drink sounded like a good option about now.

"Get your case. You know where the guest room is. Just throw it in there. I'll call Bernie to get everyone rounded up. They bring the best food since that catering place opened with the daily specials. I'm putting the coffee on now."

Little flashes of my life kept sneaking out. I hadn't had coffee in *how* long? I was keeping my cool, but felt oddly nervous at the same time. What the hell was happening? Did the *Twilight Zone* really exist? Why wouldn't she listen? I was yelling my answers at her.

She noticed the suitcase standing at my feet. A frown creased her forehead. Her magnified eyes blinked. "Probably the remodel threw you for a loop, huh? I just love it. I'll have Bernie show you the way when he gets here. You don't look so good. Do you need a lie-down?"

This time I shouted at the top of my lungs. "Who are you? I'm not who you think I am." There are a ton of Chrises in the world.

She looked as if she had been slapped in the face. She pressed very close to me, those enormous brown eyes piercing my brain. "You were so nice when you were little, Chris. Please compose yourself. That stay in the hospital was the last chance to straighten up your act. Sit down. You are breaking my heart."

I grabbed my suitcase and left. Walking as fast as I could, I made it to the middle of the next block when someone else called, "Chris?"

Not again. I started to run. A car pulled up, cutting me off. The man driving said, "Excuse me. I thought you were someone else." I kept walking, and he kept following. "I'm Bernie, Marie's nephew. You look like our cousin, Chris. I think she confused you with him. He got himself sent to a rehab a year or so ago and she hasn't been the same since."

I stopped to get my breath. "She wouldn't listen to anything I told her. I'm sorry. I just had to go."

Bernie smiled. "I'm sorry too. Could I drive you somewhere for coffee?"

I sighed. "Is there a bar?"